I, DRED SCOTT

SHELIA P. MOSES

I, DRED

SCOTT

*A fictional slave narrative
based on the life and legal precedent
of Dred Scott*

*With a foreword by
John A. Madison Jr.,
great-grandson of Dred Scott*

Illustrated by Bonnie Christensen

MARGARET K. MCELDERRY BOOKS
New York London Toronto Sydney

I dedicate this book to Dred Scott and his wife, Harriett, whose lives changed the course of the history of slavery.

I also dedicate this book to every man, woman, and child who was born, lived, and died as a slave, and to those who were freed from slavery.

You are not forgotten.

CONTENTS

FOREWORD

When I first found out that Shelia Moses was writing a book based on the life and times of my great-grandfather, Dred Scott, I must say I was not sure about how it would turn out. I knew she had written Dick Gregory's autobiography, but Mr. Gregory was alive to speak for himself. My great-grandfather died without ever even learning to read or write. His wife and children were denied the right to any form of education. None of them had ever recorded their journey to freedom. How would Shelia Moses write about them and tell their story?

It occurred to me later that how she did it was not as important as simply telling his story. And she does tell his story—not the story of a court decision or a slave, but rather the story of a man, a husband, a father; and, yes, my great-grandfather.

My grandmother Lizzie Scott was Dred Scott's second-born child. She married my grandfather

Henry Madison in the late 1800s, and they had a son, John Madison Sr., who was my father. All my life I have lived proudly as the descendant of a family that helped to change the course of the Civil War and the history of slavery.

Many books have been written about the Dred Scott Decision and all the judges, lawyers, and slave owners who played a part in what would happen to my ancestors. However, this book is different in that it is fiction based on facts that Shelia Moses uses to give depth to the story of my forefather and his family.

This book holds true to my great-grandfather's life; my great-grandmother's support; and my grandmother and her sister, who sat on the sidelines, probably in fear.

I hope that people all over the world will read and love the characters to which Shelia Moses has given so much love. I hope you will finish this book knowing that Dred Scott was different from the court ruling that said he was only one-fourth of a man. He was my great-grandfather—and the start of our legacy.

—John A. Madison Jr., great-grandson of Dred Scott

I, DRED SCOTT

1

I was born in Southampton, Virginia, some where 'bout 1799. I ain't got no ways of knowing my right age, 'cause I was born a slave. No mamma, no pappa, and I do not know if I have a sista or brother on God's earth. If I do I would reckon they live right down the road from the Blows' plantation, where I lived long time ago. Or maybe they was taken away and ain't no telling where they is now.

Saying I do have some folks, I bet they wonder every day where I be. Just like I wonder about them. Maybe they do not exist at all. Could be they are only in my dreams. Could be they are the prayer that I pray.

It is also my prayer that if they exist they have not suffered the horror of slavery like me. I hope some nice white folks freed them years ago and they lives up north. Maybe they in a place far away like Canada. I do hope they are not still slaves back in Virginia, where my life with the Blow family started long time ago.

My Massa, Massa Peter Blow, told me he was born in Southampton, Virginia, 'round 1771. I ain't got no memory of ever belonging to nobody other then he and his wife Miss Elizabeth Blow. It's safe to reckon they bought me when I was nothing but a youngster. Maybe straight from my mamma's warm body that I ain't never laid my eyes on. I don't know what she looked like. Lord, I do not even know the color of her skin. I do not know if she worked in the fields or in her Massa's big house. Don't know nothing. The Blows is the only family I ever know anything about and they not my own.

Miss Elizabeth say she married Massa Blow in the year 1800. Never asked her about where she came from. Maybe she from Southampton too. She was a little bitty woman with long blond hair. So long that she sat on her braid when it was not pulled up in a roll. Miss Blow didn't say much of nothing and it's 'bout right that Massa was surely the boss around there.

Them Blows was as nice as any white folks who owned your soul could be. They feed me well and didn't beat on me like a dog. To my knowing they didn't beat on none of they slaves. They gave me two pair pants and a shirt each year. Every other year they gave me a new coat come winter time. Don't seem like much, but I hear tell of other slaves right down the road from the Blows' plantation going naked until they was twelve years old. Some slaves never owned a coat in they life.

The Blows was not real rich white folks, but they had enough money to own a 860-acre plantation and five slaves: Solomon, Miss Hannah, William, Luke, and I, Dred Scott.

Solomon was the oldest slave, but he picked more cotton than William and Luke put together. William and Luke was brothers and they was bought by Massa Blow when they was young just like me. They did not know they mamma and pappa neither, but at least they had each other.

Miss Hannah was a pretty woman that none of the men bothered one bit. I do not believe she ever knew her folks neither. I reckon Miss Hannah was not much older than me, but she acted like an old, old woman. Maybe she was that way because she had to take care of everyone in the Blow family. I never saw them mistreat Miss Hannah. They just worked us both hard day and night.

It was just so much to do around that old place. I think most plantations was bigger, but the Blows' home place is the only one I ever stepped foot inside of in Virginia. From the time my feet touch the floor in the mornin' until I went to bed at night I did what the Blows told me to do. Whether it be washing, folding clothes, even fanning Miss Elizabeth when she was hot in the summer time, I reckon I done it all. Except the cooking.

Miss Hannah done all the cooking. She got to sleep in the big house too. I remember her hands most of all. Maybe because they made the best biscuits I ever eat in my slave life. Miss Hannah must have had a lot of white blood because she was a light-skin woman with hair as straight as Miss Elizabeth. All her hair was tucked under a head rag most of the time and she wore old clothes that Miss Elizabeth did not want no more. She was some kind of good to me. She was a mommy in some ways. I is going to always miss and love Miss Hannah for what she done for me.

Sometimes when I was mad, I would say all kind of bad stuff 'bout Massa. Miss Hannah would say, "Hush up, boy, 'fore Massa sale you to another plantation. Hush, 'fore you get us all sold off." I did like Miss Hannah told me and I never had any trouble from the Blows. I kept my lips so tight around the Blows that I never even got sent to the fields to work.

Them other men slaves worked out in the

fields for Massa Blow until they couldn't see each other come evening. The summer months was real hard for Luke, William, and Solomon. That is when they had to chop the weeds out of the cotton while the crops was young. The days was long and at night they would hardly sleep from the mosquitoes out in the small row houses where the fields hands slept. Come fall things was not better for fields hands. They picked cotton until dark.

No matter how little money Massa Blow made from the cotton, he planted some every year.

Times was hard, but Massa Blow kept us all working and fed.

I don't know if he did it for us or himself. Honestly, Massa could not afford us slaves, but it made him feel like other white folks. It let the other white folks around Virginia know that the Blows wasn't too poor. We was counted as they property just like they land or they cows in the fields. I can't read one line, but Miss Hannah said that Massa even wrote our names down in a little black book that he kept in the kitchen drawer. Beside our names, Miss Hannah said he wrote how much we all was worth to him. She could not read either, but Hannah heard a lot of white folks talk when she was serving they supper every night.

In 1812 Massa Blow went off to fight in a war. Miss Elizabeth said it was the Sixty-fifth Virginia Militia that he joined and that Massa Blow was a lieutenant there for a few years. He left me in the big house to tend to Miss Elizabeth and they little children. Just me, Miss Hannah, and Miss Elizabeth was there in the house with the children. To me, a slave, I thought Massa was a crazy man to leave us there to take care of his folks. I will never understand how white folks that hold you as a slave could trust you with they wife and children. He trusted us more than I would have if I was a white man. If I was a Massa I would think them slaves wanted to take some revenge one of these days. But not Massa, he did not think like that at all. He didn't think we would hurt a soul. It was like he knew we would not run off.

Massa was right. We had no where to run to.

When Massa came home, he went back to his business of farming and I kept up my business of the housework with Miss Hannah. Massa complained almost every day that things just were not going good with the crops. He said that money was low.

Lord, when it rained, the fields would be full of water. Most of the crops would drown in a day or two and nothing made Massa Blow madder than losing cotton, peanuts, or anything else he was trying to grow. Soon he started talking about us all leaving Virginia.

It musta have been fall when we moved because all the fields hands were called in from picking cotton so that Massa could give them the news. Massa Blow said we was moving to a new plantation near a place called Huntsville, Alabama. Massa told me and the other slaves that Huntsville was about four hundred miles from Virginia. There he said the land was higher and the crops would not drown from all the rain like in Virginia. I reckon I was about eighteen when Massa sold his farm and we all headed south to our new home place.

By then the Blows had themselves six children: Miss Mary Anne, Miss Elizabeth Rebecca, Miss Charlotte, Miss Martha Ella, Mr. Peter, and Mr. Henry. They was not mean children, just a little spoil. But they did not treat me too bad. I was older than them, but I played with them to keep them happy and out of Miss Elizabeth's way 'round the house.

It was me and Miss Hannah's job to do all the packing and loading wagons for our long trip to the new plantation. When we was done packing, we headed south. Miss Elizabeth, Massa, and the children was in one wagon, the furniture in two wagons, and the slaves and food in another one. To my knowing I left no folks behind.

The trip must have taken a month or a little over. We went through places I had never heard of 'fore—North Carolina, South Carolina, and Georgia. My Lord, all the way there I would see cotton fields filled with slaves picking cotton from sunrise to sunset. Seem like the farther south we went the more slaves I saw. When we stopped along the way, I stayed close to the wagons. I stayed close to Massa Blow. I was scared that some overseer from another plantation along the way would take me for a runaway slave and I would end up belonging to someone else. Worse than that, I would be sent into fields every day to be worked like an animal. I heard tell it happen to many slaves while traveling south. Sometimes overseers would come in the middle of the night and steal slaves while they Massas slept.

When we finally arrived in Huntsville, me and Miss Hannah did all the unpacking and taking care of the children while Miss Elizabeth got rested up from the trip. Massa Blow put the fields hands to work right away. There was so much cotton to chop the weeds out of. The farm was not much bigger than the one in Southampton, but it was more land than house. More land for the poor fields hands to work in.

It did not take long for Massa Blow to

figure out that farming was hard in Alabama just like in Virginia. So hard that we only stayed there two years 'fore Massa Blow came home one day and said we all was moving again. This time to a place called Florence, also in Alabama.

Things in Florence just was no better than they was in Huntsville, and after near ten years Massa Blow just got tired of one bad crop after another. In 1830 he came home and said we was all moving to a place called St. Louis, Missouri.

Massa Blow and Miss Elizabeth sat they children down and told them all 'bout this state of Missouri. They had eight children now. Two more boys, Mr. Taylor and Mr. William, was born in Alabama. I listened at the door so I would know something about this strange place that they was taking us to next. Massa Blow said it was a trading post that folks out there called "Gateway to the West." Massa Blow said that they trade everything from furs to slaves there. I could tell by the way he was talking that my Massa was not sure one bit what he would do in that place, St. Louis. That scared me some kind of bad. If he did not know what he was going to do, then what would he do with five slaves? Soon we all would know.

2

The trip to this new place called St. Louis was gonna take us ten long days and nights. Took me and Miss Hannah longer than that to pack our belongings.

I still remember seeing St. Louis for the first time. Before you see St. Louis, you see the Mississippi River. That river run along the edge of St. Louis and white folks are everywhere on that riverfront. I could not stop looking at the slaves loading and unloading the ships. They were loading furs, animals, and there were more slaves than I had ever seen at one time. Loading them to be sold in the South. Right 'fore my eyes, ships was loaded with slaves and headed south for them to be sold away from they mammas, they daddies, and they children. It was a sad sight to see.

After I got Massa Blow, Miss Elizabeth, and the children settled in, I walked the streets in St. Louis, doing different errands for Massa, but never after dark and never without papers in my pocket saying that I belonged to Massa Blow.

I learned that not far away from the river-bank, over on Locust Street, was a place called Lynch's Slave Pen, owned by a white man named Bernard Lynch. Massa Blow told me to stay as far away from that place as possible. He said soon as they caught his back turned, someone would think I was a runaway. A runaway that they would sale for about five hundred dollars. Some runaways was kept at the pen until their Massas came to get them. If no

Massa came for them, they were sold to only God know who or where. Other slaves were there because they Massas did not need a slave no more or they Massas just needed the money. On Sixth Street, a short ways from Bernard Lynch's Slave Pen, was another slave market owned by a white man named Corgin Thompson. I tried to stay as far away from both places as much as possible.

But one day my misfortune took me closer to Locust Street than I ever wanted to be. Closer than I ever want to be again. There was slaves everywhere: men, women, children, and small babies. White folks who had just bought them was tearing babies right out of they mommies' arms. The babies were sold to one Massa and they mammas to another Massa. When the auction was over, the Massas made them poor slaves head toward the riverfront, all in chains, crying like they life was over. Maybe they life was over. Who knows where they ended up. But sure as the day is long, they never saw they kinfolks again.

Other slaves said that they heard stories about some slaves jumping off the ships into the Mississippi River to die in the bottom of the muddy waters. They would rather die than be sold south or be taken away from they kinfolks. I prayed night and day that the Lord would not let me end up on that slave ship.

No slaves or white folks wanted to go south after word spreaded to St. Louis about a slave named Nat Turner. Through different white folks we learned that he was from Southampton, Virginia, and that he went on a killing rage one night and killed white women, men, and children in that area. Massa Blow even said that his old plantation was only eight miles from the plantation where Nat Turner lived. I heard fear in Massa voice for the first time in my life.

White folks never let us slaves know what they scared of, because they want to keep us scared all the time. But I know good and well Massa Blow was thinking about how glad he was not to be in Southampton when that Nat Turner killed all them white folks. I know he was glad he moved to St. Louis.

It seemed like white folks in St. Louis had more money than Massa Blow. They said Massa Blow was "slave poor." That's what white folks called other white folks who had more slaves than money or white folks who owned no land.

The Blows was just average white folks trying to take care of they children. We were not in St. Louis too long before Massa Blow rented a big house on Pine Street right off of Main Street from a white man named Peter Lindell for twenty-five dollars a month. Quickly he turn the new rented house into a boarding house and called it the Jefferson Hotel. He said the white folks coming and going while trading on the riverfront would need a place to lay they heads at night.

Before we could get ourselves settled into the Jefferson Hotel, on July 24, 1831, the worse thing that a man could imagine happen to Mr. Blow. Miss Elizabeth died at forty-six years old and broke every heart in that house. She wasn't sick long and she died quietly in her bed with all the children and Massa Blow standing 'round her. It was some kind of sad. I don't know what killed Miss Elizabeth at such a young age, but seem like Massa was never the same after that. He talked about her like the poor lady was still 'mong us living. I do not believe he looked at another woman, not even a supper date, after Miss Elizabeth was dead.

The only thing that seemed to make him

smile again was when his oldest gal named Miss Charlotte got herself married off in the winter of 1831 over at the First Presbyterian Church to a man named Joseph Charless Jr. Mr. Charless had plenty of money because his daddy, Joseph Charless Sr., was the man who started that newspaper called the *Gazette Missouri* in the earlier years. I heard Massa Blow tell some of the white boarders at the Jefferson Hotel that the *Gazette* was the first newspaper west of the Mississippi. On top of the money he already had, young Mr. Charless was a lawyer. And when young Mr. Charless married Miss Charlotte, he and his daddy had already opened the finest drugstore in all of St. Louis. Miss Charlotte had plenty money.

Many marriages would follow in the Blow family after Miss Charlotte's big wedding. In 1833 the oldest Blow boy, Mr. Peter, married Miss Eugenie LaBeaume. Her folks was right good and rich too. Her brother Charles Edmund LaBeaume was a lawyer. Two years later, in 1835, Miss Martha Ella Blow, the youngest gal, married Charles Drake, who was a lawyer too.

But it was Miss Charlotte's marriage that I believe changed my life forever. I do not know if it is so, but Miss Hannah said that Massa Blow sold me to pay for Miss Charlotte's wedding. Others say I was sold to catch up the bills at the Jefferson Hotel after Massa Blow had to pay for Miss Elizabeth's funeral. In 1831, for whatever the reason, I, Dred Scott, was sold just like a piece of furniture.

3

Lord, I was so scared of belonging to a new white man that when Massa Blow told me I had been sold to Massa John Emerson, I ran away. I went over to where us slaves called Lucas Swamps on Twelfth and Pine Street and hid for days. It wasn't really no swamp. Just a place for us slaves to go to get away from white folks. We cooked outside and played cards and other games together. Just a place to be away from our Massas. A place that we could go and feel like real men, not slaves.

My old Massa Blow sent Miss Hannah to get me and she told me to go on over to my new Massa's house. Didn't have to worry about white folks coming for me because that was a spot that white folks never came because it was dirty and dark. Didn't nothing happen to me for running away 'cause Massa Blow told my new Massa where I was and that Miss Hannah would get me for him.

"Ain't no harm down in the swamp," Miss Hannah told them both. "Dred just scared. I'll get him for you."

Next thing I know Miss Hannah was down there looking in my face. After she talked to me, she went back to the Jefferson Hotel to Massa Blow and I went on over to Massa Emerson. I didn't feel like a man no more, felt like my old self again, a slave!

That is what I was to my new Massa Emerson, just another slave. He was a doctor who wanted mighty bad to be a army doctor. In September 1832 he got his wish when he got a job for one month at a place called the Jefferson Barracks, just south of St. Louis. He was hired by a man named Brigadier General Henry Atkinson after the other white doctor at Jefferson Barracks got real sick. So Massa Emerson took the job and left St. Louis right away.

While Massa Emerson was far away, he hired me out to many different white families. Of course, Massa keep all the money that they paid for my services. That one month that Massa Emerson was suppose to stay in Jefferson Barracks lasted for nearly a year until General Atkinson finally found a doctor that he wanted to keep on permanently. On October 25, 1833, Massa Emerson was told he would be moving to a place called Fort Armstrong, Illinois, and he finally got his wish again. Massa was appointed to what they called assistant surgeon in the army of the United States. He had to be in Fort Armstrong by December 1. He came home to pick up some of his belongs, including me. This new place Massa Emerson said was about three hundred miles away from St. Louis. We left St. Louis on November 19.

Before I left, I got the bad news about my old Massa Blow. I did not see him much, but I kept up with his coming and going through his other slaves. It was one of his slaves that told me that Massa Blow done died the summer before and I didn't even know it. On June 23, 1832, my old Massa had met his maker. And Miss Hannah, God rest her soul, died the same summer. It made me some kind of sad to hear about Miss Hannah dying and Massa, too. Compared to my new Massa, Massa Blow was a nice white man, even if he did sale me to pay his bills or for Miss Charlotte's wedding.

Miss Charlotte's marriage turned out to be a blessing for the younger Blow boys after Massa Blow went on to glory. Two of the Blow boys, Mr. William and Mr. Taylor, went to work at Mr. Charless' drugstore and that was good for them with no daddy and all. Later on they became Mr. Charless' business partners at that same store.

All and all the Blows was pretty nice folks. But I had to forget about the Blows, because Massa Emerson owned me now.

I wasn't in Fort Armstrong long before I realized that place was worse than living on a plantation back in Virginia. There were other Negroes at Fort Armstrong; some were free, but most of them was slaves like me. They were body servants to their masters just like me. One of the servants who had been there a long time told me that the government allowed each officer one servant and that they paid for their clothes and food.

The thing about this place called Fort Armstrong that was different from St. Louis was the way white folks didn't live much better than us Negroes. Massa Emerson complained every day about what he called "poor living conditions" in the cabin that was suppose to be used as a hospital for the white folks in the army. Massa Emerson old log cabin where he slept in at night had holes in the ceiling and it leaked every time it rained. My sleeping place was even worse. Just a old blanket on a dirt floor in a small wooden cabin. When it rained in Massa place, it poured in mine. It's a wonder we did not all get some dreadful disease and fall dead.

Soon the white folks replaced Massa

Emerson run-down one-room log cabin that he slept in with a nice tent. And they gave him new tents for hospital rooms. By then, Massa had got some disease in his foot and couldn't even wear a shoe. He asked to be sent back to St. Louis, but the army would not send him back. It wasn't long before all the troops, the Massas, and the body servants were moved to a new place called Fort Snelling out in the territory of Wisconsin. The year was 1836.

It was there in Fort Snelling that I met a slave girl named Harriett Robinson. She did not know for sure, but she thought she was 'bout fifteen at the time. She did not have a lot of words to say. She just smiled and did what she was told by her Massa. She belonged to Major Lawrence Taliaferro, who owned more slaves than anybody else there. I started to love Harriett as much as a slave trying to love a woman would love anyone. Hard to love a woman when you know she could be sold away from you any time and any day. I just prayed to the good Lord and took my chances. In 1837, I asked her to marry me and she said yes.

Surely enough the good Lord was listening and Major Taliaferro sold Harriett to Massa Emerson for reasons only God knows. They even let us have a real wedding just like white folks. Major Taliaferro did the marrying because he was the justice of the peace for the whole army base.

Most of the time slaves didn't have no wedding. They just got another slave to say a few words for them and then they jumped over the broom, like they grandfolks did back in Africa. After Major Taliaferro said what he wanted to me and Harriett at our wedding, we was real husband and wife.

For the first time in my life, I had someone to love me. I had me someone to love.

Now we were both Massa Emerson's slaves. We took care of him and from time to time Massa hired us out to a white woman named Catherine Anderson. Miss Catherine treated us all right and paid every dime we made to Massa. All we got was food, a place to sleep, and clothes to wear.

Not long after I married my Harriett, Massa came and told us that the army folks wanted him to move back to Jefferson Barracks. Massa said the water was just too low for me and Harriett to travel in the boat with him on the Minnesota River, so he left us behind to work for lots of other white folks while he went by canoe to Jefferson Barracks in October of 1837. Don't remember who all we done work for in that time, but I remember good that Harriett worked for Lieutenant

James Thompson for a little while and she worked for Major Joseph Plympton, too.

It wasn't long before we got word through other slaves that overheard they Massas saying that Massa Emerson had moved again. Yep, before Massa could even get his bags unpacked at Jefferson Barracks, the army sent him to Fort Jesup, Louisiana. South!

Lord, I was some kind of glad that I was not with him. No colored man, free or a slave, wanted to go south. Some free men would go south with their freedom papers and white folks would catch them, beat them, tear up all their freedom papers, and make them their slaves.

While Massa was down in Louisiana, he met a man named Captain Henry Bainbridge. Captain Bainbridge's wife, Mary, had a sister named Irene Sanford, who married Massa

Emerson. After he got married, Massa Emerson sent for me and Harriett to come down there with him and Miss Irene. We got down to Louisiana by boat and from that day on, we had two Massas—Massa Emerson and his new wife.

Massa was complaining about that place just like he complained about all the others. Nothing was ever good or clean enough for Massa Emerson. Guess he complained a time too many, because the army sent us all back to Fort Snelling. The truth be told, I was 'bout sick of Massa complaining and nagging folks all the time. I was sick of his telling me how bad things was for him. Wonder what he would do if he was a slave. Then he would really have something to complain 'bout.

All his complaining is what got us all sent to Fort Snelling. On October 21, 1839, we all arrived back in Fort Snelling on a boat called the *Gipsey*. This time we had another person with us. Me and Harriett had ourselves a baby gal named Eliza. It was a mighty joy to have a child of our own. Now we prayed night and day that our Eliza would never be taken from us and sold to another white family. Before Eliza was born, we used to pray that we was never sold away from each other. Now we had to pray to keep our Eliza with us.

To the best of our ability we all tried to make the most of Fort Snelling. One day Massa asked the Quarter Massa to provide me with a stove so that I could do all the cooking and he and Miss Irene would not have to eat in the mess hall no more. When the Quarter Massa told Massa Emerson no, Massa up and went crazy. He just started fussing and cussing at the poor man. The

Quarter Massa was a little man who just upped and hit Massa in the face and broke Massa Emerson's glasses. Now that was something I had wanted to do for a long time, after all his nagging me and Harriett. Massa Emerson was so mad that he walked away and came back with a gun and the Quarter Massa ran off. When the commander found out what Massa Emerson done, he was not happy one bit and he ordered him down to the Seminole War in Florida in May 1840.

I would reckon that Miss Irene was tired of moving by now, so Massa Emerson went to Florida by himself and sent us all back to Missouri to live. Miss Irene lived out at her daddy Alexander Sanford's plantation called the California. The California was a lot bigger than any plantation I had lived on before and it was not too far from St. Louis. She hired us out to different white folks in St. Louis right away to make money for her own pockets. Most of the time we worked for Miss Irene's brother-in-law, Captain Bainbridge.

By now me and Harriett had ourselves another baby. We named her Lizzie. Miss Irene was some kind of mad because she would only get four dollars a month for Harriett now. My Harriett, she could not work as long anymore with two children to care for. Some of the time Harriett had to take the children to work with her and white folks did not like that at all.

Finally, in 1842, Massa received a dishonorable discharge from the army and came home to Miss Irene and to be our Massa again.

White folks in St. Louis did not take too kind to Massa anymore. All the tales of him moving around had caught up with him and white folks were not sure he was a good enough doctor. Once again Massa left Miss Irene out at her daddy's plantation and he went to the Iowa Territory to be a private doctor for the folks there. Massa came home from time to time, but for the most part he stayed in Davenport, Iowa, until he got sick and died on December 29, 1843. By then he and Miss Irene had a baby of their own, a gal named Henrietta. Massa Emerson was forty years old when he died. Their gal was only one month old. The poor child never even got to know her daddy.

After Massa died, Miss Irene stayed out at her daddy's plantation for good and we worked there from time to time. Mostly, Miss Irene kept us hired out to work for Captain Bainbridge or other white folks in St. Louis. We hardly ever saw her after a few months. I guess you would say that me, my wife, and our children were slaves with no Massa.

At least we thought that until we tried to buy our freedom from Miss Irene.

4

We was away from Miss Irene to make money for her and she was not about to give us our freedom now. She continued to hire us slaves out to Captain Bainbridge, who then hired us out to Samuel and Adeline Russell in March of 1846. They owned a store called Russell and Bennett's over on Water Street.

Around that time Harriett started going to church more and more, taking Lizzie and Eliza with her. I went from time to time, but my Harriett and the girls never missed a Sunday and sometimes they went during the week nights. In those days there were only two churches for colored folks in all of St. Louis. Harriett 'tended Second African Baptist Church. Before we had them two churches, colored folks went over to Liberty Engine House at Third and Cherry Streets. Before Liberty Engine House, black folks met at each other house.

After church let out, black folks would stand around for hours and talk about how they could get they freedom. Some of them worked and saved money and bought they freedom when they Massa didn't want slaves after leaving the South. Another way slaves was being freed was if they was born to a free black woman and they could prove it. A few was freed because they had sued they Massa for taking them into free states on they way to St. Louis from the South.

Without telling a soul except Harriett, I

had saved enough money over the years to buy our freedom. Miss Irene frowned at me something awful when I told her that I wanted to buy our freedom. Then she said "NO."

That made my Harriett real mad.

One Sunday Harriett came home and told me that she been talking to folks at church about all the places we had been with our Massa Emerson. When they heard about our travels, folks at the church told my Harriett that she was not a slave no more. They told her that me and the children was not slaves no more. They talked about something called the Missouri Compromise. Harriett said it meant that slaves who was born into or was carried into any territory north or west of Missouri was not slaves no more. That's what happen to me and my Harriet. We was carried into the free state of

Illinois and the free territory of Wisconsin and had worked there as slaves.

Reverend Anderson told Harriett he had somebody he wanted us to meet—someone who would help us because of that Missouri Compromise law. Someone he said could get us our freedom, like him. Yes, Pastor Anderson was a free black man. He was a big man, who mamma was a slave brought to St. Louis from Virginia. Don't know when his mamma died, but he worked and bought his freedom long before me and Harriett met him. He even learned to read and write from the white folks. He took us to meet a man named Francis B. Murdoch, who was a slave lawyer.

Pastor Anderson and Francis Murdoch both used to live in Alton, Illinois. Reverend Anderson use to be what they called a type-setter over in Alton for a man named Elijah

Lovejoy. Mr. Lovejoy went and got himself killed trying to help slave folks. He had lived in St. Louis first and he was publisher of the *St. Louis Observer* newspaper and he was pastor of Presbyterian Church.

The St. Louis folks decided they had enough of Mr. Lovejoy when he started writing about the murder of a free black man named Francis McIntosh, who was a steward on one of the steamboats. One day when the boat was docked in St. Louis, the sheriff and some of his deputies tried to arrest a free Negro man from the boat and Francis McIntosh stepped in to stop them. A big fight broke out and Mr. Murdoch killed one deputy and hurt another one. He was arrested right away and put in the city jail. When night came, them white men dragged him out of that jail cell. They dragged him over to Tenth and Market Street where they tied him to a tree and set him on fire and burned the poor man to death. Mr. Lovejoy did not think it was right for Francis McIntosh to kill a man, but he said it was wrong for them to burn the man to death. He wrote about it all the time until he got so many death threats that he left St. Louis for good and he moved to Alton.

But that did not stop Mr. Lovejoy from writing about the wrong that was done to slaves. Two times the mad white menfolks tried to burn down his *Alton Observer* printing shop in the middle of the night. Folks said in November of 1837 Mr. Lovejoy got himself a brand new printer. Mr. Lovejoy, Pastor Anderson, and some other men stayed at the shop day and night to keep the mad white folks from destroying it like the other one. Pastor Anderson said they guarded that printer with they lives. But on November 19, a whole mob of angry white men showed up and tried to take the new printer.

Mr. Lovejoy and his men were ready for them and they had a shoot-out right there in front of the printing shop. They hurt a few of the men, but they shoot Mr. Lovejoy five times and killed him dead. Not only that, Pastor Anderson said they took the printer and threw it in the Mississippi River.

Lawyer Murdoch was the city attorney over there in Alton and he tried real hard to put the men who killed Mr. Lovejoy in jail, but the white folks in town was glad Mr. Lovejoy was dead and they did not support Lawyer Murdoch trying to bring justice for his murder. Soon after that, Lawyer Murdoch and Pastor Anderson moved back to St. Louis.

Lawyer Murdoch told us all about Mr. Lovejoy and how many slaves he helped. He said he was going to help us to get our freedom from Miss Irene. He said that if everything we said was true, and we had really gone to Illinois and Wisconsin, then we was free people. Lawyer Murdoch went on and on about us having the right to go in that courthouse down on Pine Street and ask the judge for our freedom. Night after night me and my Harriett talked about what the preacher and the lawyer said to us.

Free! Me and my Harriett was free Negroes and we didn't even know it.

Lawyer Murdoch said he would be our lawyer if we wanted him to and he would go over to the old courthouse and help us get our freedom. On April 6, 1846, that is what he did. He marched right into that courthouse and sued Miss Irene Emerson for our freedom. Me and Harriett could not read a word on his papers, but Lawyer Murdoch said he ask the court to charge Miss

Emerson with false imprisonment. He said that false imprisonment meant Miss Irene was holding us for her slaves and we were free people. Free just like her.

White folks and the law agreed that slaves could not be married, so they didn't even include my Harriett's name on the court papers when that whole mess started. Lawyer Murdoch said that the man at the courthouse wrote my Harriett's first name and started to write her last name, but he crossed it out. Slave men had no rights, but slave women had even less. I reckon Harriett's name should have been on every last one of those papers from start to finish. But Lawyer Murdoch said if we won, none of that would matter and we would get ourselves ten whole dollars and our freedom. That money we would get was what he call "damages." He said damages was payment for mistreating people.

Harriett was scared for the children after we filed our suit, so different abolitionist started to keep them hid 'round St. Louis for us most of the time. Abolitionist was them white folks that was against slavery. Not just for me and Harriett, but for all people. Surely Miss Irene was mad about this. Harriett thought she would be mad enough to try and sale off our children, but she never did.

Lawyer Murdoch said that Deputy Henry Belt rode all the way out to the California plantation and put them courthouse papers into Miss Irene's hands. Lord, I wish I would have seen her face when that horse came up with the deputy on it. I wish I could have seen her eyes reading them words.

Miss Irene was supposed to wait to come to court in November to tell the judge why she had been keeping us as slaves when we was free people. But not Miss Irene, no sir, she didn't wait one day. She went right out and got herself a lawyer named George Goode. He went over to the courthouse the next day and did what Lawyer Murdoch called answering the charges against Miss Irene.

Surely enough, me and my Harriett had a visitor of our own the next day. Sheriff Milburn did not even send a deputy; he came himself with papers for me and Harriett. We couldn't read the papers, so we ran to Lawyer Murdoch's office. After he calmed my Harriett down just a little bit, he read the papers to us. "Take notice that on the ninth day of April 1846, I shall move the court to dismiss the suit of yourself against me for your freedom." He said that meant Miss Irene had ask that the charges against her be dismissed because she said that

Lawyer Murdoch did not even pay what they call a bond to cover the cost of court. We didn't understand any of that legal mess he was telling us. But I did understand him when he said Miss Irene was just trying to stop us from getting our freedom.

That day was the beginning of eleven long years of trying to be what we had already been for many years. Free!

I barely slept all them nights as we waited for Lawyer Murdoch to go back to court for us. But he never made it to court for us. Pastor Anderson came in the alley where we lived one day and gave us the bad news. Before we went to court in 1847, Lawyer Murdoch just upped and moved all the way to California without saying one word. Now we had a day in court almost here and we had no slave lawyer to even talk for us. Till this day I still do not know why Lawyer

Murdoch left St. Louis. Truth is, we do not know if he ever left for California. Some white folks believe he was killed for trying to help us get our freedom.

The Lord mighty good because I went and found the only white folks in St. Louis that I knew could help us. The Blow boys! I told them all about Miss Irene and Massa taking us into free states and how Lawyer Murdoch told us we was free. I told them about Lawyer Murdoch moving to California and leaving us high and dry. Just like I thought, they told us they would help us get our freedom.

Thank God their sister Miss Martha Ella had married Lawyer Charles Drake. He told the Blow boys that he would be glad to be our attorney. He started doing the paperwork, but then Miss Martha Ella died and Lawyer Drake was so heartbroken that he move away to Cincinnati. Before he left, he ask a lawyer named Samuel Bay to help us.

On June 30, 1847, Lawyer Bay went to the court house for my Harriett and me. When he came back, he say we still was not free and that there would be another trial for us on the second day of December. By now Miss Irene done got real mad and she went to a bigger court over in St. Louis and tried to stop Lawyer Bay from going to court for us again come December. Miss Irene did stop us for a little while, but Judge Krum said the case would be heard come January and sure enough it was. For the first time in our lives, on January 12, 1848, that same Judge Krum told Lawyer Bay we was now free people.

Miss Irene was not having no such mess and on that same day she ask the judge for another trial. Lawyer Bay called it an appeal and he said he had to go back to court for us and he did. This was getting to be too much for Lawyer Bay so he got some help from two other attorneys named Alexander Field and David Hall. They went to Judge Krum and asked for a new trial. This time the trial would be over in Jefferson City, where they had the Supreme Court.

While we waited for them new lawyers to go over to Jefferson City for us, Judge Krum put us in the hands of the sheriff to hire us out to work for other white folks. The Blow boys was mighty upset about this so they asked Charles Edmund LaBeaume, who was Peter Blow's wife Eugenie's brother, to hire us. Mr. LaBeaume didn't really need no help, though, so often times he would hire us out to other white folks. But always to good white folks.

We was working for a lot of different folks when we got the word that the judge over in Jefferson County said we was not free. So me, my Harriett, and our children were slaves again. Again our lawyers asked for an appeal.

But on May 17, 1849, everything for slaves, free colored folks, rich and poor white folks changed. A big fire started on a steamboat that was docked at the riverfront and spreaded onto land when the wind got real high. It burned down half of downtown St. Louis in just a few hours. After the fire was under a little control, folks just walked around in a daze for days. To make it worse for us all, the cholera broke out and folks in St. Louis started to get sick and die by the dozens. After that no one wanted to come into the city for no court date for some slaves like us.

A lot of people black and white died

from that cholera, even our old attorney Samuel Bay.

It was not until January 12, 1850, that we got a new trial. By now Miss Irene had herself new lawyers named Hugh A. Garland and Lyman Norris. Lawyer Field and Lawyer Hall was still our lawyers.

All of this was too much to understand, but when we got to the new trial the judge did what the lawyers called a "overturned verdict" and he freed us again. Not only was we free, but the judge said we had been free ever since we stepped foot in free territory sixteen years ago.

Our freedom was short-lived because Miss Irene went right back over to Jefferson City and asked for another trial and they gave her one. On February 13, 1850, she got what she asked for and we were slaves again.

I never did understood why Miss Irene wanted to keep us as her slaves, because she didn't even live in St. Louis no more. In 1850 she married a man named Dr. Calvin Chaffee, who lived all the way 'cross country in a place called Boston, Massachusetts. She left her brother John Sanford, who came back and forth to St. Louis from New York, in charge of the case.

The sheriff hired me out to one family and my Harriett to another. For the first time in our lives we had no Massa, but we was not free neither. And then we had no lawyer because David Hall died in 1851 and Alexander Field left St. Louis to be a lawyer in Louisiana.

Again our Blow friends helped and asked Mr. Charles LaBeaume to ask his good friend Roswell Field to be our lawyer. I was working for Lawyer Field at night cleaning

his office over at 36½ Chestnut at the time.
Lawyer Field was not my Massa. He had
hired me from Charles LaBeaume, who had
hired me from the sheriff five years earlier
for five dollars a month. Seem like everything was changing again.

Lawyer Field said it was just fine if John
Sanford took over Miss Irene affairs because
he was from New York. I ask Lawyer Field
what difference did it make to us where Mr.
Sanford lived. He said it made all the difference in the world to a judge, because if a person who lived in another state sue someone
in St. Louis, then it's a federal case.
"Federal," he said, could give us the right to
sue in court all the way in Washington, D.C.,
if need be. There in Washington, D.C., he
said was a group of judges called the
Supreme Justices, in the highest court in all
the land. He was sure they would give us our

freedom. Before that, Lawyer Field said he would try again in the federal court in Missouri over in Jefferson City.

Twice that federal court told Lawyer Field "NO" to letting us have a new trial. Lawyer Field told us that the only thing left to do was to go to Washington, D.C. He wrote Lawyer Montgomery Blair, who was a good lawyer who lived in a big mansion right across the street from the White House in Washington, D.C. At first Lawyer Field got no answer from this Lawyer Blair. So Lawyer Field wrote him again and Lawyer Blair wrote him back and said he would go to the Supreme Court for us. He did and on March 6, 1857, a man that Lawyer Field said was the chief judge, Justice Roger Taney, read from a fifty-page paper what that Supreme Court had decided to do about my Harriett and my children and me. Lawyer Blair wrote and told Lawyer Field that it took that man two long hours to say what he had to say. He also wrote that not one person left that courtroom the whole time Judge Taney was reading.

The news that took two hours to read was bad. The judge said that we was first from Africa and no one with any African blood was a citizen of the United States and we had no rights like white folks to even sue in the United States courts. But Lawyer Field said what knocked white folks off they feet was the judge said the United States Congress was wrong for ever making the Missouri Compromise a law. And he said the judge said that law was now nullified. Lawyer Field said that "nullified" meant it was no longer the law. Seven of the judges agreed with this Judge Taney. But two did not.

Lawyer Field said it were over and there was no other court to go to. No more judges that would listen. After eleven long years, we was still slaves.

5

My Harriett cried something awful and I just hurt mighty bad for us all.

We was still in the hands of the sheriff because Mr. John Sanford died on May 5, 1857. Before he died, he give us back to his sister, Miss Irene, in his will. And it turn out that Dr. Chaffee didn't even know his wife, Miss Irene, owned us when he married her. He was a abolitionist just like that Elijah Lovejoy. The good folks in Massachusetts was upset with Dr. Chaffee when they read in the paper that he and him new bride was slave owners.

The Blows never stopped caring about us and helping us and they wrote to Dr. Chaffee as soon as they heard he didn't want no slaves no more. Dr. Chaffee was all too happy to sale us back to Taylor, the son of my first Massa Peter Blow. Taylor was a boy I once played with and he was the man who finally freed me. He freed my Harriett, my Lizzie, and my Eliza, too. Dr. Chaffee probably would have freed us himself, but Lawyer Field said that there was a law that say you cannot free your own slave if he or she did not stay in the same state with you. So he had to sale us to Taylor Blow back in St. Louis to free us.

Don't know where Lawyer Field was that day. But on May 26, 1857, his partner, Lawyer Arbu Crane, drew up our freedom papers and went over to the court house with us and Taylor Blow to see Judge Alexander Hamilton, who gave us our freedom forever.

I was tired something fierce, but I was free!

News about our freedom was in newspapers all over the country. The next month Lawyer Field told us that even that man Abraham Lincoln who was running for president of the United States of America spoke about us in one of his speeches. This man named Lincoln said that we was human being, just like a white man, and we should be free. That was some kind of special. Made me feel like a man.

After we was free, Lawyer Field helped me get a job at the Barnum Hotel over on Second and Walnut Street and my Harriett washed and ironed for white folks. In the evening when I got off work, I would take the clean clothes to the white folks. I would bring home a whole basket of dirty clothes for her and my girls to wash, iron, and fold.

One day my Harriett was washing and the girls was ironing when someone came knocking at the door.

"Who that?" Harriett called out as I went to the back of our small place to hide. Harriett always wanted me to hide when white folks came by. She had heard a lot of white folks talking about taking me north to make money. They believed some whites in the North would pay a whole lot of money just to see the slave whose case went all the way to the Supreme Court in Washington, D.C. Said they would even pay me a thousand dollars a month. That money did not mean nothing to Harriett as bad as we needed it. She said we would make a good living as free people just like anybody else. The other reason she didn't open the door was because folks was trying to get a picture of me. My Harriett believed it was bad luck. She said that taking our picture was like stealing our spirits.

"Who that?" Harriett yelled again.

"Is this where Dred Scott lives?" A voice that sound like a white man yelled back.

Harriett got mighty mad, but she open the door. There stood two white men, not one.

I came out before Harriett told them folks a piece of her mind.

The men were reporters who wanted to do a story about us and they talk to us a long time about having my picture taken at the Fitzgibbon Gallery. Harriett just kept on telling them people no until finally they told her they would take her picture and the girls'. The girls really wanted their picture taken, so Harriett finally broke down and said "Yes."

The next day we all got dressed in the

best clothes that we had and left our place in the alley and headed over to the Fitzgibbon Gallery. The walk was not that long, but it always took us a long time to get around the city, because folks was always stopping us to talk. Everybody wanted to see the slaves that white folks was making such a fuss over.

When we got to the gallery, one by one they took our picture. When we finish, we all went back home, with our spirits. Free spirits.

AUTHOR'S NOTE

Dred Scott died on September 17, 1858, of what many believed was tuberculosis. Three days later the *St. Louis Evening News and Intelligencer* ran an article with news of Scott's death:

> The somewhat eminent Negro known as Dred Scott whose name is intimately connected with perhaps the most famous and important decision the United States Supreme Court ever rendered, died in this city last Friday. He was born in Virginia and was

brought to this city by Captain Peter Blow, father of Henry T. and Taylor Blow, to whom he originally belonged. His last owner was Rev. Mr. Chaffee of Massachusetts, who got possession of him by marriage, and by whom he was emancipated soon after the last Supreme Court decision. Dred was a good-natured, harmless, faithful Negro, and was about fifty-seven years old at the time of his death.

Dred Scott was buried at Wesleyan Cemetery, formerly located in what is now the St. Louis University campus; when that cemetery closed, his remains were removed to an unmarked grave in Calvary Cemetery, Section 1, Lot 177, in north St. Louis County by the man who freed him, Taylor Blow.

In 1957 Father Edward Dowling (now

deceased) tried to raise enough money for a headstone for Scott's grave. Taylor Blow's granddaughter made a donation large enough to cover all costs.

Dred Scott's headstone reads as follows:

front:

DRED SCOTT
BORN ABOUT 1799
DIED SEPT. 17, 1858
FREED FROM SLAVERY BY HIS FRIEND
TAYLOR BLOW

back:

DRED SCOTT BORN ABOUT 1799 DIED SEPT. 17, 1858
DRED SCOTT SUBJECT OF THE DECISION OF
THE SUPREME COURT OF THE UNITED STATES
IN 1857 WHICH DENIED CITIZENSHIP TO THE
NEGRO, VOIDED THE MISSOURI COMPROMISE
ACT, BECAME ONE OF THE EVENTS THAT
RESULTED IN THE CIVIL WAR

No one really knows what happened to Harriett Scott or where she is buried. Their daughter, Eliza, had no children, and she died at the age of twenty-five in 1862. The whereabouts of her remains is unknown. Her sister, Lizzie, married Henry Madison. When and where the couple died or where they are buried is unknown. They had seven children. Some of the descendants of those children still live in St. Louis, Missouri.

THE IMPACT OF THE DRED SCOTT DECISION

The Dred Scott Decision served as an eye-opener to Northerners who believed that slavery was tolerable as long as it stayed in the South. If the decision took away any power Congress once had to regulate slavery in new territories, these once-skeptics reasoned, slavery could quickly expand into much of the western United States. And once slavery expanded into the territories, it could spread quickly into the once-free states. Lincoln addressed this growing fear during a speech in Springfield, Illinois, on June 17, 1858:

"Put this and that together, and we have another nice little niche, which we may, ere long, see filled with another Supreme Court decision, declaring that the Constitution of the United States does not permit a State to exclude slavery from its limits. . . . We shall lie down pleasantly dreaming that the people of Missouri are on the verge of making their State free, and we shall awake to the reality, instead, that the Supreme Court has made Illinois a slave state."

For many Northerners who had remained silent on the issue, this very real possibility was too scary to ignore. Suddenly many Northerners who had not previously been against the South and against slavery began to realize that if they did not stop slavery now, they might never again have the chance. This growing fear in the North helped further contribute to the Civil War.

Four years after Chief Justice Taney read his infamous *Scott v. Sanford* decision, parts of the proslavery half of the Union had seceded and the nation was engaged in civil war. Because of the passions it aroused on both sides, Taney's decision certainly accelerated the start of this conflict. Even in 1865, as the long and bloody war drew to a close with the Northern, antislavery side on top, a mere mention of the decision struck a nerve in the Northern Congress. A simple and customary request for a commemorative bust of Taney, to be placed in a hall with busts of all former Supreme Court Chief Justices, was blocked by the Republican-controlled

Congress. Charles Sumner, the leader of those who blocked the request, had strong words on the late Chief Justice and his most notorious decision:

> "I speak what cannot be denied when I declare that the opinion of the Chief Justice in the case of Dred Scott was more thoroughly abominable than anything of the kind in the history of courts. Judicial baseness reached its lowest point on that occasion. You have not forgotten that terrible decision where a most unrighteous judgment was sustained by a falsification of history. Of course, the Constitution of the United States and every principle of Liberty was falsified, but historical truth was falsified also."

Clearly *Scott v. Sanford* was not an easily forgotten case. That it still raised such strong emotions well into the Civil War shows that it helped bring on the war by hardening the positions of each side to the point where both were willing to fight over the issue of slavery. The North realized that if it did not act swiftly, the Southern states might take the precedent of the Scott case as a justification for expanding slavery into new territories and free states alike. The South recognized the threat of the Republican party and knew that the party had gained a considerable amount of support as a result of the Northern paranoia in the aftermath of the decision. In the years following the case, Americans realized that these two mindsets, both quick to defend their side, both distrustful of the other side, could not coexist in the same nation. The country realized that, as Abraham Lincoln stated, "A house divided against itself cannot stand. . . . This government cannot endure, permanently half slave and half free." Scott's case left America in "shocks and throes and convulsions" that only the complete eradication of slavery through war could cure.

"The Impact of the Dred Scott Decision"
by Lisa Cozzens, May 25, 1998

CHRONOLOGY

1799

Dred Scott is born in Virginia as a slave of the Peter Blow family.

1803

The United States purchases the territory of Louisiana from France.

1804

The U.S. takes formal possession of what is now Missouri.

1820

Congress admits Missouri as a slave state. The question of Missouri statehood sparks widespread disagreement over the expansion of slavery. The resolution, eventually known as the Missouri Compromise, permits Missouri to enter the U.S. as a slave state along with the free state of Maine, preserving a balance in the number of free and slave states. The Missouri Compromise also dictates that no territories above 360–30' latitude can enter the union as slave states. Missouri itself is located at the nexus of freedom and slavery. The neighboring state of Illinois had entered the union as a free state in 1819.

1830

The Blow family moves to St. Louis.

1831

Dred Scott is sold to John Emerson.

1831-1842

Over the next eleven years Scott accompanies Emerson to posts in Illinois and the Wisconsin Territory, where Congress prohibits slavery under the rules of the Missouri Compromise (a law of which Scott is not aware).

1843

John Emerson dies. Irene Emerson hires out Dred, Harriett, and their children to work for other families in St. Louis.

1846

Dred and Harriett Scott sue Irene Emerson for their freedom in the St. Louis Circuit Court.

1847

The circuit court rules in favor of Irene Emerson.

1850

In a second trial the jury decides that the Scotts deserve to be free, based on their years of residence in the nonslave territories of Wisconsin and Illinois.

1852

Irene Emerson appeals the decision to the Missouri Supreme Court. The state supreme court overrules the circuit court decision and returns the Scotts to slavery.

1853

Scott files suit in the U.S. federal court in St. Louis. The defendant in this case is Irene Emerson's brother, John Sanford.

1856

Scott and his lawyers appeal the case to the U.S. Supreme Court.

1857

Irene Emerson remarries. Since her husband opposes slavery, she returns Dred and his family to the Blow family. The Blows give the Scotts their freedom.

1858

Dred Scott dies of tuberculosis and is buried in St. Louis.

1860

Abraham Lincoln is elected president in a political contest that is dominated by the discussion of slavery. South Carolina secedes from the Union, and the Civil War begins.

BIBLIOGRAPHY

Cozzens, Lisa. "African American History: The Dred Scott Case." http://www.watson.org/~lisa/blackhistory/scott/index.html (May 25, 1998).

Ehrlich, Walter. *They Have No Rights: Dred Scott's Struggle for Freedom.* Westport, CT: Greenwood Press, 1979.

Founding.com. "Abraham Lincoln's Speech on the Dred Scott Decision—June 26, 1857." http://www.founding.com/library/1body.cfm?id=321&parent=63 (August 6, 2004).

Kaufman, Kenneth C. *Dred Scott's Advocate: A Biography of Roswell M. Field.* Columbia, MO: University of Missouri Press, 1996.

ACKNOWLEDGMENTS

In 2001 I met a wonderful man whose friends and family called him Wink. I met Wink while he lay dying in the hospital. He was an interesting man who greeted everyone with a smile and his famous line, "Hello, earth angel."

These are my earth angels: my mother, Maless Moses; my siblings, Barbara, Daniel, Johnny, Scarlett, Larry, Leon, Loraine, Gayle, and Jackie; Eric Goins; April Russell; Ray Johnson; Deborah Rogers; Rebecca Franklin; Judge Myra Dixon; Kim, Elliott,

Trey, and Eric Abnatha; Marie, Ronald, Ron Jr., and Katie Showers; Sonia Sanchez; Morgan Freeman; Shelia Frazier; Barbara Austin; Paul Benjamin; Melvin Van Peebles; Nick LaTour; Dick and Lillian Gregory; my editor and friend, Emma Dryden, and all the wonderful people at Simon and Schuster; my agents at McIntosh and Otis and my former agent, Tracey Adams; and my lawyer and gatekeeper, Darryl Miller.

I love you all. . . .

ABOUT THE AUTHOR

Poet, author, playwright, and producer Shelia P. Moses was raised the ninth of ten children in Rich Square, North Carolina, where her highly acclaimed novel *The Legend of Buddy Bush* is set. She is the co-author of Dick Gregory's memoir, *Callus on My Soul,* and she resides in Atlanta, Georgia.

Margaret K. McElderry Books • An imprint of Simon & Schuster Children's Publishing Division • 1230 Avenue of the Americas, New York, New York 10020

FIRST EDITION

Every effort has been made to locate all persons having any rights or interests in the material published here. Any existing rights not herein acknowledged will, if the author or publisher is notified, be duly acknowledged in future editions of this book.